Arthur Yorinks's
The FLYING LATKE

with
Art by
William Steig

PHOTO ILLUSTRATIONS BY
PAUL COLIN & ARTHUR YORINKS

SIMON & SCHUSTER BOOKS FOR YOUNG READERS

Author's Note

With the finished manuscript of *The Flying Latke* in front of me, I knew that this would be a difficult book to illustrate. Broad farce is hard to contain within the confines of the standard thirty-two page picture book format. So it occurred to me: Why not simply "stage" the story, illustrate it as one might stage a play?

William Steig graciously agreed to supply the "backdrops"—the background art. I then began to design the book by arranging the text, and Paul Colin and I created a rough layout of the illustrations. I "cast" the book with actors and friends, and Paul and I digitally photographed them in Paul's studio in New York. Using Steig's art as a guide, I positioned the actors in what I hoped would be the correct poses so that each person would be "blocked" in the right place. With more than 800 photographs to sort through, I chose the most appropriate, and Paul and I, with the aid of the computer, composited the photographs into William Steig's wonderful interiors. The result is the book you are about to read.

Many people aided and collaborated in this "production." I'd like to extend special thanks to Alex Ferrari, senior designer at Cezanne Studio, as well as all those without whom this book could not have been created.

SIMON & SCHUSTER BOOKS FOR YOUNG READERS
An imprint of Simon & Schuster Children's Publishing Division
1230 Avenue of the Americas, New York, New York 10020

Book design by Paul Colin and Arthur Yorinks
The text of this book is set in 17-point Sabon.
The background art is rendered in watercolor.

Printed in the United States of America

2   4   6   8   10   9   7   5   3   1
Library of Congress Cataloging-in-Publication Data

Yorinks, Arthur.
The flying latke / by Arthur Yorinks ; illustrated by William Steig. —1st ed.
p. cm.
Summary: A family argument on the first night of Chanukah results in a food fight and a flying latke that is mistaken for a flying saucer.
ISBN 0-689-82597-8 (hardcover)
[1. Hanukkah—Fiction. 2. Jews—United States—Fiction.] I. Steig, William, 1907- , ill. II. Title.
PZ7.Y819Fl 1999
[E]--dc21 98-37712
CIP
AC

'm telling you, my family was nuts. Cuckoo. Totally meshugge!
All right, all right, so maybe they're still a little meshugge, but you
should have seen them last year. You think I'm kidding? Here, here's
a picture.

Nu? Every day it was something else. This one didn't get along with that one. Someone wasn't speaking to someone else. The fights. The arguments. You shouldn't know from it.

But then, I know it's hard to believe, a miracle happened. What, you don't think they happen? Sure, they happen. Maybe not so often, maybe once in a blue moon — but look, see for yourself.

It all started on the first night of Chanukah. The whole family was over. You know, Uncle Izzy, Aunt Sadie, Uncle Shecky, Aunt Etta, Aunt Esther, Uncle Al, Aunt Shirley and, oh yeah, all my cousins: Nettie, Lettie, Howard, Sy, Sidney, Sol, Wolfie, Murray, Marvin, Tillie, Roberta, Pauline, and Bob.

Anyway, my mother doesn't believe in appetizers, so there we
were, standing around, starving, when finally my mother hollers,
"Dinner!" Like bandits, we all ran into the dining room.

"Izzy," my mother said as she brought in her prized platter of latkes. "It's Chanukah, it's Chanukah, come light the menorah." But Izzy—Izzy was busy. Busy arguing, of course.

"What are you saying," Izzy shouted. "I know cars, I know Fords, and that one was a Ford."

"It was a Buick," my uncle Shecky bellowed.

"A Ford!"

"A Buick!"

"A FORD!"

Shecky, fit to be tied, picked up a pickle and waved it at Izzy.

"Izzy," Shecky said, shaking the pickle, "you wouldn't know a Ford if it was sitting in your driveway with the dealer's sticker on it!"

"A sticker?" Izzy said.

"A sticker!" said Shecky as he gave the pickle one last shake and, well, you guessed it. The pickle took off like a rocket and hit Izzy right in the forehead.

"A *sticker*!" Izzy yelled. "I'll give you a sticker!" Izzy picked up the salad bowl and dumped it on Shecky's head.

"Izzy, please," cried Sadie. "Not in front of the children!"

"Sadie," Shecky announced. "Izzy could throw all the food on this table, all the food we had at Esther's wedding, including the five kinds of melon balls, and still, *still* the car that cut us off would be A BUICK!"

That was it. The food flew. The chicken, the borscht, the sour cream, the bread, even the chocolate Chanukah gelt. In no time, there was nothing left. Nothing but a few latkes and the largest one was in Izzy's hand.

"Izzy," my mother pleaded. "Not the latke. It's Chanukah."

But Izzy was Izzy.

"I'll show you a Buick!" he said. His wrist gave a flick and the latke went flying.

"YAAAAAAAH!" everyone screamed as the latke flew over Shecky's head and out the window into the night sky.

I raced to the window to see where the latke would land and, well, I know this is weird but, it didn't. I mean, it didn't come down. The latke just kept going.

"You're happy? You're happy now?" my mother said to both Shecky and Izzy. "My whole dinner, that I slaved over—"

"Sylvia," my father said to my mother. "Calm down. Everybody calm down. Come. Let's all go sit in the living room and cool off. We'll sit. We'll watch TV."

Most of the time, when my father talks, nobody listens. But this time, who knows why, we listened.

We shuffled into the living room and Sidney turned on the television. We sat. We shmoozed. Suddenly, we heard the following:

"WE INTERRUPT THIS PROGRAM TO GIVE YOU A NEWS BULLETIN. A UFO HAS JUST BEEN SPOTTED FLYING OVER THE NEW JERSEY TURNPIKE," said an anchorman from the six o'clock news.

"IT IS A SMALL OBJECT," he continued, "AND ALREADY THERE IS SPECULATION THAT WE JUST MIGHT BE ENCOUNTERING VISITORS FROM ANOTHER PLANET. THIS COULD BE A MOMENTOUS MOMENT FOR HUMANITY. LUCKILY, WE HAVE SOME VIDEOTAPE TAKEN BY A SALESMAN IN TRENTON. LET'S TAKE A LOOK."

Our eyes were peeled on the TV when my aunt Etta shrieked, "It's the latke! It's the latke!"

It was the latke. My mother's latke was flying over New Jersey.

"You see, you see, you had to throw it out the window," my mother complained to Izzy.

The news bulletin continued: "THE AIR FORCE HAS NOW CONFIRMED THE SIGHTING OF THE UFO AND HAS MADE SEVERAL ATTEMPTS TO COMMUNICATE WITH THE OBJECT. BUT THERE HAS BEEN NO RESPONSE. THIS COULD BE A SIGN OF HOSTILE INTENT. IN FACT—WAIT, THIS JUST IN. A DECISION, FROM THE WHITE HOUSE, HAS BEEN HANDED TO THE AIR FORCE. THEY WILL TRY TO SHOOT DOWN THE UFO."

"My latke!" screamed my mother. "Morty, they're going to shoot my latke! Call the police, call the President!"

"Sylvia, please—"

"MORTY!"

What could he do? My father picked up the phone and called the first air force base he could find. It was in Maine.

"No, colonel, it's a latke!" my father yelled into the phone. "Izzy threw it out the window and—no, latke. L-A-T . . . No, look, it's a potato pancake for Chanukah. CHANUKAH. C-H-A . . . No, no, it's a holiday. You know, the Maccabees, against all odds, defeated the . . . no, MACCABEES. M-A-C . . . Listen here, who are you calling a crackpot? Oh yeah, well, you're a crackpot. You're the one that's shooting missiles at a potato pancake!"

My father slammed the phone down. My mother started to cry. Aunt Sadie had to lie down.

"You had to throw the latke," Esther yelled at Izzy. "Look at what you're doing to your sister. What's the matter, a piece of celery wasn't good enough?"

"Look, Esther, maybe if Sylvia had served a little something when we got here—"

"Oh, oh, now it's my wife's fault," my father joined in. "I haven't seen Sadie cook a meal since Irving moved to Long Island."

"Morty!" Sadie cried. "When was the last time *you* picked up a pot?"

The fighting went on like this for hours.

"Maybe we should go," said Shecky.

"What?" said Etta. "How can I go home after this? You think they won't find out that it's *our* latke?"

"Etta," my father said, "they don't know you had anything to do with this."

"They know," Etta continued. "Believe me, they know."

At that, the doorbell rang.

"Go see who it is, Danny," my father said.

"It's the FBI, dad," I called from the front hallway.

"Oy, I'm plotzing," shrieked Etta. "Izzy, go talk to them."

"Me? Why should I—" Izzy began. But with the look everyone gave him, he shrugged and went to the door.

Though we tried to listen, we couldn't hear the FBI men, who, by the way, were all tall. But we did hear Izzy.

"Yes, my name is Isadore Feldman," he was saying. "Yes, I make zippers for a living, a very comfortable living, I might add. What? Oh. Yes, the UFO was here, right in this house. Yes, I think it was made of potatoes."

Izzy didn't get a chance to say much more. Within minutes, the house was surrounded by a mob of reporters.

"That's it," Etta said, looking out the window. "We're not leaving here until this blows over."

"But, but we have no food in the house—" my father started to say. It was no use. Surrounded and hounded by onlookers and reporters and Hollywood producers, we were trapped in our house for days. Eight days and eight nights, to be exact.

And so tell me, tell me if what happened next wasn't a miracle. As my mother's latke flew around the world, our plate of latkes, the only food we had, which should have lasted, with this crowd, about seven and a half minutes, lasted for eight days!

Don't ask. The whole family, fressing on latkes alone, stayed and didn't argue or even hardly complained at all. Eppes, *that* was a miracle!

On the last night of Chanukah, as we looked longingly at our empty platter, suddenly the flying latke flew through the window, into the house, and landed—*boom*—right on the plate.

We all stared at the amazing latke until Izzy quietly piped up. "All right," he said, "maybe it *was* a Buick."

Shecky and Izzy hugged, Etta cried, and Esther turned to my mother, pointed to the latke and said, "Sylvia, I want that recipe!"

Yes, it was a happy Chanukah.

Amen.